T0123330

TWO QUICK READ SHORT STORIES

(Reflections with a Common Touch)

ED HARRIS

authorHOUSE®

AuthorHouse™
1663 Liberty Drive
Bloomington, IN 47403
www.authorhouse.com
Phone: 833-262-8899

Published by AuthorHouse 07/31/2021

ISBN: 978-1-6655-3383-6 (sc)
ISBN: 978-1-6655-3381-2 (hc)
ISBN: 978-1-6655-3382-9 (e)

Library of Congress Control Number: 2021915771

Print information available on the last page.

A Summer to Remember

I was at school, concerned about the Corona Virus. I was reminding the students to keep their masks above their noses, keep social distancing, and to wash their hands. It was sad to me that the students had to suffer through this difficult time. The on-line education was new for them, and most of us teachers as well. My mind started to drift back, to when I was a kid, about their age. A more peaceful time for being a kid. It was a summer to remember.

It was the summer of 1957. Dwight D. Eisenhower was president, and the United States was in an economic crisis. My Dad was in the Air Force. We were being transferred from James Connally Air Force Base in Waco Texas, to Ellsworth Air Force base, about 10 miles outside Rapid City South Dakota.

Dad and Mom had much to do to prepare for the move. This was great news for me. The plan was, to meet my first cousin Mike, and his parents, at our maternal grandmother's home. Granny, lived in our, very small home town, Louisiana, Missouri (I was born there, but left when I was around 5 years old). This was very exciting. This would be the first time I was going to be with "Granny" and Mikey, at the same time, for the entire summer.

Before we arrived, Granny had signed Mikey and me up, to play Little League Baseball. Mikey was placed on a younger level team, and I was placed on a team, that was a step above his. Mikey already knew most of the players on his team, while I knew, no one on my team.

By league rule, the coaches could schedule three practices and two, sometimes three, games a week. The teams usually played 10 games and a championship game if possible. Most of the games were played under the lights on Friday and Saturday nights. The league consisted of teams from Louisiana and teams from nearby towns.

The First Game

Even though the team had practiced about five times, in the first baseball game of the season, I was very nervous. I almost urinated on myself in warmup. I made it to the rest room, just in time. When I played on the Air Force base, there were never crowds like the one that I saw that day.

Granny and Grandpa Clifford always took Mikey and me to the games. Mikey's team played in the early game, and my team played right after. The crowd did not seem so intimidating during Mikey's game.

However, when Bobby (my new best friend) and I, hit the field for the second game, the whole team was excited. The applause from the crowd made me feel as though, I was in Busch Stadium. Busch Stadium was home of the St.

Louis Cardinals Baseball Team (The crowd actually consisted of only about 100 - 350 people). Probably every parent and grandparent, of each of the players, that could come, was at the game, cheering for their kids, and grand kids.

When the opposing team took the field, for their warmup, to me they looked bigger, stronger, and faster than our team. This was our team's first game, but it was the second game for the Bombers. The previous weekend, the Bombers had won their first game, by five runs vs. the Vandalia Hornets.

In Little League we played 7 innings, rather than the 9 played, in the big leagues. By the end of the fifth inning, the Bombers were ahead 3-0. Surprisingly, Bobby was 1 for 4 at the plate. Bobby was our best hitter, and everyone expected that he would be explosive in the game. But, not so far.

As the game progressed my competitive spirit overcame my nervousness and I could not even hear the crowd. I blocked out the noise. We were on defense again, and Royce Clayton our ace pitcher, walked the first batter he faced that inning. Royce then struck out one, one got a single, and the fourth batter hit it to me at second base.

I scooped it up, tossed it to Russell, the short stop, he tagged second, then threw it over to first for the double play. It was a beautiful play; the fans erupted with applause and praise, as we ran off the field. The Bombers did not score, it was bottom of the seventh, our last turn at bat. It was our last chance to do something to get some hits.

Every one of the starting 9 players had batted at least twice except Royce. Royce was the first at bat this time. Since Royce was the pitcher, he hit last in the lineup. The crowd was calm as Royce stepped to the plate. Royce was probably the best, all-around athlete on the team. Royce was lean, rangy and strong for our age.

When Royce connected with the ball in practice, he generally hit long singles, but he was inconsistent. Although everyone on the team was pulling for him, no one really expected that he would get a hit. A walk was the most that we hoped for from Royce.

To the surprise of Coach Patterson, and all the players on the bench, on the first pitch, Royce smashed the ball hard and it travelled over the head of the left fielder. The left fielder fell, trying to turn and chase the ball. By the time the center fielder, crossed over to cover for the left fielder, the ball had rolled all the way to the fence. Royce was rounding second base, headed to third, when the center fielder, finally got his hands on the ball.

The crowd was "going crazy" and the boys on the bench were filled with excitement and jumping around hugging each other cheering. When Royce's foot hit third base, the shortstop was receiving the cutoff throw. Our coach, at the third base coaching box, put both arms high in the air, that was the signal for Royce to hold at third.

Royce was looking toward the shortstop, and missed the signal from the coach. Royce was running hard toward home plate. The catcher was standing up to receive the throw. The shortstop flung the ball, with what seemed like all of his strength, toward the catcher. Royce and the ball got there at about the same time, there was a collision at the plate, and a huge cloud of dust.

When the dust cleared, the umpire signaled safe. The opposing coach came running off the bench screaming at the umpire that Royce was out. The opposing fans were also demanding that Royce was out. But it became obvious that the umpire was right. When the players stood, the ball lay in the dirt, where the catcher's body had been on the ground. The catcher had dropped the ball! Our bench, and our fans, erupted with cheering and excitement. This fired-up our team, we were energized!

I was the next batter and got the bunt signal. I stepped into the batter's box and waited, for the left-handed natural curve, from the opposing pitcher. The ball was coming fast, looked to be looping to my outside, but instead curved down the middle, just above my knees.

I turned my upper torso and held the bat with a hand holding each end. I bent my knees, as the ball popped off my bat up the first base line. I sprinted toward first. The pitcher was running straight toward me to get to the ball. He mishandled the ball and I was safe at first.

The opposing pitcher, who had been "throwing bullets," during the whole game, was rattled after that. He walked the next two hitters. The bases were loaded. Our team was going wild and so were our fans.

The opposing coach called time out, and walked to the pitcher's mound. We all suspected, he would replace the pitcher. But, to everyone's surprise the talk they had, was just encouragement, a "settle down" talk. Bobby stepped to the plate.

I remembered that in many of our conversations, while throwing rocks into one of the streams in Louisiana, Bobby and I talked about our favorite players. I could not decide between Jackie Robinson and Willie Mays, but Bobby was solid on Babe Ruth, but he also liked Mickey Mantle, as a current player. Bobby would talk about Babe Ruth being his all-time favorite baseball hero.

Bobby talked about wanting to have, what he called, "Babe Ruth moments." Bobby, defined a Babe Ruth moment as hitting a homerun, with enough players on base, to win the game. I had the feeling that, right then, Bobby was living, a "Babe Ruth moment."

Bobby took two strikes, then off a blistering fast ball, Bobby blasted the ball, over the left center part of the fence, for a homer. The fans went wild, the team was waiting to mob Bobby as he rounded the bases and stepped on home plate. We won 5 to 3, an amazing "come from behind" victory, especially for the first game of the season.

After the game we were all invited to meet the coach, just west of town, at the A&W Root Beer stand. When all of the players arrived, the excitement of the big win continued. The coach bought us each a large drink, 10 cents each, a hotdog 10 cents each, and fries 5 cents for each player. I realize now, that back then, the cost was about 25 cents a player, which totaled about $4.85. Also, since all seating was outside, it was probably the only place in town where everybody on the team could be served equally. Because, in 1957, the Jim Crow attitudes, of some people, were supreme.

A Friend Indeed

Bobby and I met at practice. Bobby was the starting catcher and sometimes "the closer," as a pitcher on the team, and I started at second base, but sometimes played shortstop. Bobby and I repeatedly practiced the throw, from catcher to second base. That was an important through, to practice as a Deterrence, for teams attempting steals, of second or third bases. As the season progressed, because of consistent practice, very few successful steal attempts occurred against Bobby and me. Coach Patterson said that Bobby and I were a terrific combination. We became fast friends that summer.

Bobby and I were typical 9 year old boys. Our friendship however, might have seemed a little different to some people though; because Bobby is a white boy, and I am a black boy. I am sure that it was odd, to some people, that Bobby and I, were all over town together, riding our bikes everywhere.

Bobby had sandy colored hair. He was about two or three inches taller, and probably 5 to 10 pounds heavier, and had a thicker frame than

I. Bobby was a strong kid. He probably got the size from his father, who was a tall stout looking man, about 6'5", 225 lbs. Bobby told me that his dad did a little, heavy weight boxing, when he was in the Army. I was in awe.

Although Bobby was bigger, I was faster and quicker, than he. Bobby was the home run threat on the team, and hit in the "clean-up" slot, number four hitter. I was a consistent singles hitter and sometimes doubles hitter, so I hit first in the line-up. I was also the best base runner on the team, often stealing bases to put the team in scoring position. Bobby and I had a mutual admiration society, going between us. Bobby was impressed with my speed and agility. I was amazed with his power and strength.

In 1957, Louisiana Missouri, was a safe town for kids. Therefore, our families were not worried, that we were riding around town, from place to place, during the days, largely unsupervised. Almost every adult in the town, knew to which families we belonged. The adults, kind of looked out for each kid, when kids were, in the adult's sphere of influence. Sometimes Bobby and I would leave home, on one of our many adventures, after breakfast, and not return until just before dinner. For two 9 year old boys, 1957 Louisiana, Missouri, was a place full of fun, adventure, and excitement.

Entrepreneurship

Two weeks later, Bobby and I decided to find and sell some soda bottles to earn money. Bobby and I discovered, that if we rode our bikes over to the city parks, early Monday mornings, there were often trash cans full of empty soda bottles. People, after picnics, held over the weekend, had tossed their empty bottles away. We realized, that we had to get there, before the trash pickup, so we had to move quickly. Bobby brought a couple of burlap sacks from his home, in which to carry the possible loot.

On that particular Monday morning, the first Monday, after the 4th of July holiday, we hit the jackpot. We found 67 empty soda bottles in various trash containers around the park, a real treasure. We filled our bags with about 33 bottles each.

We propped the bags of bottles against the handlebars, and the middle bar on our bikes. We rode very carefully to the corner store. The store was about a mile away. When we arrived at the store with so many bottles, Mr. Stewart the store owner, was impressed.

Mr. Stewart paid us two cents each for the bottles, $1.34 total. As a bonus, Mr. Stewart gave us a nickel each. He wanted to encourage us to continue to bring empty bottles, very lucrative for his business. We were sure that we were "rich." Bobby and I divided the money in half. Adding in the nickel bonus, we then had 72 cents each. We agreed to meet at the movie theatre on Saturday morning to spend our new found wealth.

On Saturday when Bobby and I met at the movie theatre, it looked like every kid in town was there. The cost of a ticket was forty cents. Inside at the concession stand, we both purchased a large bag of popcorn, a candy bar, a large fountain soda, and a hotdog.

The total cost for the movie and snacks was about $.70 for each of us. Once we collected our purchases at the concession stand, Bobby started toward the main auditorium door. Bobby motioned for me to follow. I started toward the doorway, just then, the usher moved over to block my way. Bobby saw this occur and immediately came to my defense.

Bobby said, "Hey, what are you doing?"

Pointing at me the usher said, "He can't go into the main auditorium."

Bobby defiantly asked, "Why not?"

"He's colored. Colored people aren't allowed. They have to sit in the balcony."

The usher pointed to the stairs to the left of the main auditorium doors. The usher, with a crooked smile on his face, continued his explanation to Bobby.

"If you want to sit with the coloreds, you can just go on up to the balcony with him."

As Bobby started to walk toward the stairs with me, he turned to talk to the usher again.

"That is the stupidest rule I ever heard!"

"I don't make the rules Kid; I'm just doing my job."

As Bobby and I walked, up the stairs to the balcony, I could sense the anger rising in him. He said, more talking to himself than to me.

"This is so dumb. This is really dumb!" Bobby looked straight at me and asked, "Are they trying to say colored people are not as good as white people?"

I was confused by his question. He had grown up in Louisiana all of his life, I asked myself; had he not noticed that there were no black people on the school buses? Had he not noticed the separate restrooms and water fountains in the stores? Did he not notice that black people were not allowed in the restaurants in town? My answer was short, but not entirely truthful.

I softly said, "I guess so."

The truth was that I knew full well what was going on. This Jim Crow situation was a definite down - side of life, off the Air Force Base. Jim Crow was not welcome, on military bases, especially after Executive Order 9981, issued by President Truman, in 1948, desegregated the military. It seemed that Bobby could sense that this conversation was uneasy for me to talk about with a white boy.

Actually, I was very worried about hurting Bobby's feelings. He seemed to be genuinely naive concerning the realities of Jim Crow. As we took our seats, Bobby and I "went silent" for a while. The cartoons, newsreel, cliffhanger, and two movies we saw, were not as enjoyable, as we hoped they would be. We could not get the incident, in the lobby, off our minds. Also, the incident in the lobby, put a damper on everything else that happened that day.

Lunch Date

One day before practice, Bobby invited me to his home for lunch. It was the first time I had been invited into the home of a white person. We rode our bikes up the hill most of the way, but the hill was so steep, that we eventually had to get off, and push our bikes the last quarter mile or so, up the hill. When we were, almost to the front door, we leaned our bikes against the small concrete front porch.

I followed Bobby as he moved around the front steps and crossed the brick sidewalk that connected to the driveway. Bobby did not use the front door, but lead me between the truck and the house, to take me in through the side, screen-door. I noticed the writing on the door of the truck, Olindorf Hauling and Contracting. As soon as Bobby walked through the door, he went over to kiss his mother and hug his father, both were standing in the kitchen.

"Hi Momma and Daddy, yawl probably remember Jimmy, from the ball games. He plays second base."

Bobby's dad reached out to shake hands with me. Smilingly he said, "Yeah, he is a hell of a ball player. Come on in, have some lunch with us."

To me Bobby's dad looked huge. I had seen him at the games, but he was always sitting in the stands, cheering for the team. But now that he was standing across from me, he was definitely a big man. My hands were dwarfed by his large mitts, as I shook hands with him.

Bobby's Momma moved over to give me a hug. She smiled and said, "Yes, we remember

Jimmy from the games, and you talk about him every day at dinner." She looked at me and said, "Welcome young man. Have a seat at the table."

Bobby's mom, turned and looked at Bobby, she told him to slide over on the bench seat at the table. That arrangement caused Bobby and I to sit next to each other. Mrs. Olindorf yelled toward the other room.

"Dabney, come on Honey, lunch is ready."

"Ok Momma, I'll be right there."

The kitchen looked cozy. The table was in the center of the floor, it looked like a wooden park table. There was a long bench on one side, and two wooden chairs on the other side. Also, wooden chairs with armrests were at each end of the table.

The iron stove had four burners. A big sink, and an "ice box" was to one side. A long counter was on the opposite side of the stove, with cabinets and shelves above and below. On the walls were photos of current and, I assumed, deceased family members.

A very large American flag, also hung on the wall. The flag was painted on small wooden planks, pieced together, like a large puzzle, encapsulated in a large wooden frame. The flag was in the center of the wall, behind the two chairs at the table. U.S. Army paraphernalia were also in several spots along the wall.

Dabney came through the door headed for her seat at the table. Love hit me like a ton of bricks, when I saw her. She was gorgeous! I had to force myself not to stare at her.

Dabney's long, dark brown, almost black hair, was parted to one side, and fell to the small of her back. Her hair seemed to frame her dimpled, round face, and dark blue eyes. Dabney was about 5'3" and slender. She looked very athletic, maybe due to the fact, that she was a freshman cheerleader at the high school. I had an immediate crush on her.

As she sat in her chair, she looked at me, smiled and said, "Hi, you must be Jimmy. So, great, you're having lunch with us today; welcome."

I was shocked that she knew my name. I was still staring at her. I realized, I really needed to say something to greet her in some way. She actually smiled at me. I felt embarrassed. I was hoping, no one noticed that I was blushing. I looked down at my plate and said, "Hi," so low almost no one could hear. I could see Mr. and Mrs. Olindorf sneak, knowing glances, and smiles at each other. Mrs. Olindorf tried to save me, as she passed around the hamburgers, hotdogs and potato salad.

"I heard that your Dad is in the Air Force?"

"Yes Ma'am."

"So, are you here in Louisiana visiting someone."

"Yes Ma'am, my Granny Louise and Grandpa Clifford."

Something I said seemed to stir the curiosity of Mr. Olindorf.

"Oh, is your Grandpa Clifford the driver and handyman for Dr. McCarthy? Dr. McCarthy lives in one of those big houses over on Georgia St.?"

"Yeah, I think so."

Mrs. Olindorf said, "Oh yeah, I know Dr. McCarthy! He is the head of Pediatrics over at the hospital. His father was Chief of Surgery before he retired several years ago."

I asked, "Do you work at the hospital?"

"Yes, I worked with Dr. Andre in Pediatrics for years before I moved over to the Emergency Room."

"Dr. Andre? My cousin Mikey's middle name is Andre, he was named after the doctor, that was there when he was born. Could Dr. Andre have been the same person? I think he was my doctor at birth too."

Mrs. Olindorf looked surprised, she looked more deeply at me as she spoke.

"Wait a minute, are you Ms. Louise Hill's grandson?"

"Yes Ma'am."

Mrs. Olindorf told us all about her work with Dr. Andre and being at my birth and Mikey's birth. She knew my mother, and my aunt and uncle. She knew that my father was away on duty in the Air Force, when I was born.

It was very interesting, listening to her talk about my family. It was like she knew all about us. I was amazed at her familiarity with my family. Mrs. Olindorf even knew that granny, also worked for the McCarthy family. Granny was their maid. She took care of the kids, and the cooking and cleaning there.

The conversation during that delicious lunch, moved around the table with levity and friendliness. Dabney told us all about cheerleading practice, and the two "Really nice," football players, that she wanted to meet. But she was sure they had not noticed her. Mr. Olindorf asked her the names of the boys, and she told him Chuck and Sam.

Mr. Olindorf asked, "Do you mean Chuck Spitowski and Sammy Bell?"

I discovered during lunch that Mr. Olindorf was a community sport booster, for little league, and high school sport teams. He was especially interested in high school sports, and knew most of the players on the varsity football team.

Mr. Olindorf smiled and asked, "Aren't those guys seniors?"

It was Dabney's turn to blush, she said with a smile, "Yes, and that is why I am only interested in being friends with them." She sighed as she looked down and said, "They would be too old, for me to actually think about dating one of them."

It was clear that Dabney was probably, clandestinely floating the idea past her parents, to see what they would say. They were very non-committal, just looked at each other, smiled and said nothing. Dabney did not really ask a question, so her parents did not offer an answer. I was sure, no one at the table believed Dabney, was not interested in dating Chuck or Sam.

At the time, I could not stop myself from staring at her. I realized that she was an "older woman" and there were other complications of course. But it was a wonderful fantasy. Everyone in the Olindorf family, seemed very nice and made me feel welcome.

They had a big brown and white fluffy cat named "Fluffy" that frequently jumped up on the counter tops. They also had a very friendly light brown and black dog named "Sparky." Sparky looked like he was mixed with many breeds, but he looked a lot like a Labrador Retriever in the face. Even the Olindorf pets, were enjoyable to be around. That was a good lunch and nice first experience, being in the home, of a white family, that lived off base.

Talking with Granny

When I got home that evening, I told granny all about having lunch over at Bobby's house.

She asked, "Is that your friend, that plays on your baseball team?"

"Yes Ma'am."

I told her about the great meal, and how nice everyone was. I told about Fluffy and Sparky, and I told her all about Dabney. Granny listened with some coy amusement, especially when I was talking about Dabney. Granny realized how tender feelings engulf a first crush.

Granny asked, "Where does Bobby live?"

"He lives across the highway up the hill from Culpepper."

"Really? What is Bobby's last name?"

"Olindorf."

"His mother and father must be Mrs. Christine Olindorf and her husband Buddy. She was your nurse, when you were born, Mikey's too. Nurse Olindorf and Dr. Andre, were so nice to us,

27

during the pregnancies of your aunt Lucy, and your mother Mayme. That is why your Aunt Lucy, gave Mikey the middle name Andre."

Remembering that time, made Granny smile. That must have been a happy time for everyone in the family. She continued to reminisce.

"The Olindorf's were quite a couple back then. The rumor was that they met while in the Army."

I was surprised, "She was in the Army too?"

"Yes, both met when, she and he, were young officers stationed at Ft. Leonard Wood, in Pulaski, Mo. She told us that she, joined the Army right after she graduated, from nursing school."

Granny talked on about the Olindorf's. Granny seemed to be talking more to herself than to me at the time. She was very content with her thoughts of the Past. Granny seemed, not to be really thinking about the fact, that I did not have background knowledge, of what she talked about. But it was fun listening to Granny talk about it, she seemed happy.

Playoffs

Our tenth game of the season was a doozy. It came down to the last two innings. The "Eagles" from Pittsville, were undefeated and were extremely confident. Surprisingly we were ahead by 2 at the beginning of the 5th.

We had lost to them by five runs, earlier in the season, on their home field. We were determined to get revenge for our only loss. We had convinced ourselves, that they could not beat us, on our home field. The Louisiana "Mules" would be, too stubborn to lose at home.

To our dismay, the Eagles began to get "fired up" and started to gain momentum. By the end of regulation time, the Eagles tied the score. The game had to go into extra innings. The rule concerning extra innings was; the team with the most runs at the end of any extra inning wins.

Because we were the home team, we took the field to play defense first.

The Mules tightened up and held the Eagles to no runs in the 8th. The Eagles stiffened, so we did not score either. The 9th inning was the decider. The Eagles scored on a one run homer by their third baseman. The players on the Eagles bench went wild. The homer made the score 8 to 7, Eagles ahead. Royce bared down and struck out the final hitter. Now the Mules had to get at least one run to stay in the game.

Our first hitter in the inning, the pitcher Royce, struck out. I stepped to the plate and hit the first pitch deep into left field, a clean single. I used my speed to turn the single into a double.

I slid into second base safe, stood and waited in hope that the next batter, would get a hit to bring me home, or at least advance me to third. Our third hitter hit a short fly ball to the left fielder, two outs. I tagged up, but I knew I could not beat a throw from the left fielder to third. I relaxed at second base. With two outs, our next hitter came to the plate with Bobby on deck. The Mules were encouraged. All of the Mules were standing at the dugout fence, they were pulling for the next hitter, Tony La Barge.

Tony was probably the third strongest hitter on the team. Tony looked a little nervous as he stepped to the plate. Tony hit the first pitch that looked as if it might be a home run, but instead was a long foul ball. The second pitch was a ball, two strikes and one ball. I tried to help by spooking the pitcher. I faked as if I would sprint toward third base. It must have worked because even Coach Patterson was alarmed. Thinking that I was trying to steal third, he yelled to me, "get back!" The pitcher, concentrating on the hitter, threw two balls in a row, one high and outside and one in the dirt. Then it was a full count, three balls and two strikes.

Everyone was cheering, the players in both dugouts were off the benches and at the railing yelling and encouraging their respective players. The third pitch came in at the knees, but inside. It could have been a ball, but Tony could not take that chance, because it could be a strike. Tony swung hard and hit the ball on the ground, just inside the third base bag. The third baseman moved fast to his right, he made a leaping stab, across his body to make the grab. It was a spectacular get. He threw the ball to first as Tony came barreling in hard.

The first baseman got his glove on the ball, but the throw pulled his foot off the base, as I rounded third, the umpire at first base yelled, "Safe." I held up at third base. The crowd went wild!

The opposing coach called time out. The first baseman was so angry he threw his glove on the ground, and threw a small tantrum, for a couple of seconds. The opposing coach was arguing with the umpire. This game was for "Town Bragging Rights," for heaven's sake. Very important!

The opposing coach appealed the call to the home plate umpire. The home plate umpire upheld the call. Again, a loud cheer went up from Mule fans. The mules had two runners, one on first, and another on third. The Mule bench was bedlam as Bobby stepped to the plate.

Bobby looked a little nervous. I was clapping like crazy, and yelling to encourage him. Bobby stepped into the batter's box. The first pitch was very high about head level, a ball. Bobby was so nervous he swung anyway. Bobby swung so hard he lost control of the bat, and it flew halfway up the third base line, and landed out of bounds.

The crowd gasped. I could see that Bobby could feel the pressure. The second pitch was over the inside corner at waste level. Bobby swung and missed. The coach was yelling, "Relax buddy, you can do this."

Bobby stepped out of the batter's box, glanced at me standing on third. I yelled out, "Babe Ruth moment, Baby, Babe Ruth moment!" Bobby smiled at me, took a deep breath, stepped to the plate and hit a homer to deep left field.

The win against the Eagles extended the season by putting us in the playoffs. Since the Mules and the Eagles were tied at 9-1, the two teams would have to face each other again. The championship game would be played a week later, at the Eagles home field.

The Boondocks People

The next week we practiced four times instead of the regular three practices. In order to get the field scheduled for a practice, the coach scheduled an early morning session on Tuesday. The early practice would not interfere with other teams. No one wanted to practice that early, so it was easy for the coach to get the field. I actually liked early morning practices, because it left the rest of the day for Bobby and me to explore.

Just as I was thinking of exploration, Bobby pointed to the mysterious dirt road that lead into the woods. The road began about 500 steps beyond the homerun fence. I told Bobby that I had never even noticed that road before.

Bobby told me, that he had never seen anyone, use that road. He said that he had heard, from some of the older, high school boys, that there were people, who actually lived back there. The high school boys called them the "Boondocks People." "Boondocks People," that sounded kind of scary to me.

Bobby explained what he had heard from the older boys.

"The teenagers told about the rumor. According to the rumor, some years ago, the younger sister, of one of the baseball players, wandered off, back there. It was during one of the late night baseball games. The high school kids said she was never found."

I looked at Bobby suspiciously.

"Do you think, that maybe those teenagers, are just making up stories. Maybe they were, just trying to scare, the younger kids? They probably think it's funny."

Bobby said, "Well let's find out, if people really live back there. Let's go check it out after practice."

"You have got to be kidding me."

"No, really. You aren't chicken, are you?"

The fact was, I was really scared, just thinking about, going down that road. Nevertheless, I could not allow my "toughness" to be challenged. My imagination was running wild. What if the people, back in the woods, really did exist? What if they kidnapped us?

I remembered about the "Kidnapping Act," called the "Lindbergh Law." I saw the review of the Lindbergh story, that told all about the "Kidnapping Act," and the "Lindbergh Law" on one of the newsreels at the movies. That particular newsreel stuck with me. I think the empathy, for the little Lindbergh boy, really impacted me.

"I am not chicken! Do you think there may be another road somewhere, that leads out of those woods?"

"I don't think so, I never heard anyone say anything about that."

During practice, all I could think about, was my anxiety, about following that road. It scared me, thinking that people, could be living back in the woods, perhaps people responsible, for hurting some little kids. I was not sure that I was as brave as Bobby, about going up that road.

I decided, just at the end of practice, that I probably should not go. I did not look forward to telling Bobby, that I did not want to go. It would probably verify, in his mind, that I was chicken. Bobby might lose respect for me, but I still thought it wise not to go.

We all called Coach Patterson, "Coach" most of the time. At the end of practice, Coach had us huddle, for a motivational talk. I loved it when Coach, got us fired up, with one of his talks.

This time however, it seemed like he was talking directly to me concerning my dilemma about going up that road with Bobby. Coach told us how proud he was of us. He talked to us about having courage and character. He reinforced his emphasis on teamwork, and sticking together, through thick or thin. He talked about having inner strength, and fighting to the end, never giving up.

Coach had us come together, for a team break, and we all yelled in unison, "Beat Eagles!" After listening to Coach's talk, at the end of practice, I felt that I could not, let Bobby down. After Coach's talk, I had to go, up that road with Bobby.

We all helped collect the equipment, and placed it in Coach's bag. Everyone took off going their separate ways. After Coach drove away in his four door 1955, Chevy Station Wagon, Bobby and I started toward the old dirt road.

Three of the players were still talking about the upcoming game. When they saw Bobby and me heading toward the old dirt road. One of the guys, Alexander Bobo (everyone called him by his last name), yelled to us.

"Hey, where are you guys going?"

Bobby shouted back, "We are going to see what is down the dirt road."

Bobo, Josh, and Tony caught up with us and Josh asked, "You guys have heard the stories about that place, haven't you?"

I said, with false bravado, "Yeah we heard."

Bobby said, "Yeah, we heard about it, but me and Jimmy think the teenagers may be trying to play a joke on us. Trying to scare us. We thought we would check it out for ourselves. We want to know if there are actually people living back there."

Bobo said, "I'm going with you guys."

Tony was excited, "Ok then, I'm going too."

Josh said, "Wait a minute you guys. Well, you know, they never found the little girl, don't you?"

Bobby, with just as much false bravado said, "Yeah we heard."

Josh started looking very scared, the blood seemed to drain from his face when he spoke, "Maybe they ate her."

We all looked at him and there was a moment of silence, then everyone started laughing so hard, we were holding our stomachs, and falling on the ground. The laughing stopped. Then Bobo looked at us and repeated the remark, "Ate her?" Suddenly, everyone was laughing again, everyone, that is except for Josh.

Josh started backing away from us as he said, "I saw it at the movies, Tarzan had to rescue, his son Boy, from a tribe of people that were cannibals."

I said, "Tarzan? You have got to be kidding me."

Tony asked, "What's a cannibal?"

Josh said, "People who eat other people."

All of us started laughing again as Josh rode away shouting, "You guys are crazy."

Bobby replied, "Alright then, let's go Mules!"

With that remark, Bobby turned to lead the group down the dirt road. Everyone mounted their bikes and started cautiously down the road. As we moved down the road, the tree line, and weed line, grew closer to the road.

Eventually, the road became more of a path. The perfectly sunny day began to cloud. The sky was getting dark, the path was getting narrow, and the courage, of we four adventurers, was waning. As the group moved forward, it became necessary to dismount and push the bikes.

Tony was first to disengage, "Guys, it looks like it's going to rain, I better be getting on home now."

I was surprised to see Tony back out. He seemed to be such a "stud" at practice, and during games, now he was quitting. But, at the same time I was questioning myself. Was Tony, right? Maybe we should all turn around and go home.

Suddenly, we heard noises in the weeds and behind the trees. The three of us stopped to listen more closely and look around.

Bobo whispered, "Did you guys hear that? What was that noise?"

I said, "Quiet, let's listen."

We started walking again, but much slower, following the path as it started to slope downward. All of a sudden two men stepped out of the weeds from behind two trees, one on each side of the path. My heart seemed to leap into my throat. I felt like I could not move.

Bobby jumped behind me, as to shield himself from the two men. Bobo started yelling, "Help, help" at the top of his lungs, as he ran back up the trail. Bobby was holding, onto my shoulders, with each hand. He was facing my back, as he yelled to Bobo, "Bobo wait for us!" Bobby and I were not moving and Bobo was well on his way, dashing back up the slight incline.

The two men looked to be older than my Granny, somewhere between forty and forty-five. The two men were about the same height, maybe 6'2" or 6'3". They were wearing thick plaid, long sleeve, button down shirts, overalls, and homemade ponchos, made of heavy plastic. Both men were wearing old, well worn, black and white basketball shoes.

They were white men with weathered, reddish, wrinkled faces. Their long matted hair, that fell below their wide brimmed, tattered straw hats, looked in need of washing. Both men had rifles slung on their backs.

One of the men said, "What hell are you, young'uns doing way out here, when it looks like rain?"

Bobby and me were so scared, we could not speak. We just stood there looking at them. Bobby's fingers were digging into my shoulders, so deep that I could feel them pressing against bone.

There was a pause and the one with the greenish colored shirt said, "Maybe they cain't talk Billy John."

Billy John stepped behind us, just as it started to sprinkle a little harder. "Y'all better come on with us down to the house now, fore ye get all wet. You lead the way Sylus."

We felt like we did not have a choice, so Bobby and I started walking down the path, following Sylus and being herded by Billy John. I could see that Billy John had a pretty significant limp, when he walked. It made me think that we could beat him running, if we sprinted back up the path.

I then thought better of that idea; they had guns; we can't out run bullets. After about 100 more yards, a small clearing emerged. We could see that the path, lead to what looked like, an old shack, cradled by four large oak trees.

We heard the dogs barking first, then saw them running toward us, as we continued to move toward the house. They looked like hound dogs of some type. Sylus told us not to be scared. He said that they would not bite, unless we started running.

I sure hoped Sylus was right, because they looked and sounded fierce, as they approached. The dogs sniffed us as we walked toward the house. It was very intimidating; I could feel Bobby shaking as he held onto me.

As we got closer, we could see the thick limbs of the trees hanging over the house. We could see that the leaves of the trees, shielded the house from the rain, as it started to come down heavier. We made it to the covered porch just in time; the rain started coming down really hard.

I wondered if they were going to kill us, like they did that little girl. Bobby whispered to me, "It's the Boondocks People." Then we were both shaking as we considered about how we would escape.

The porch was big, about 10 feet wide, and went from one end of the house, to the other. The entire area was screened in. Heavy furniture decorated the porch, made it look like a kind of rustic living room. Three rocking chairs, a table with a bench, on either side, a long sofa, with several smaller tables beside each rocking chair, and one on both sides of the sofa, completed the motif.

When we got to the house, Sylus held open the screen door for us, we all went inside. As Billy John came in, startled, I slightly jumped, as the door slammed behind him. A woman who looked to be, twice as old, as my Granny came out. She walked out of the screen door, that lead to the inside of the house.

She said, "How many times do I have to tell you boys, not to slam that door, damn it?"

Billy John said, "Sorry Momma. It slipped; it's wet out here."

"Well, do not come in this house with those wet clothes on."

As if startled, the old lady suddenly noticed Bobby and me. She looked at us with curiosity. It was as if she was visually examining us. She said almost in a whisper, "well, well, well," where did you find these two?"

All of a sudden, I remembered Josh. I was thinking that she was probably looking at us, as her next meal. Maybe she was sizing us up for dinner. She looked at us, then asked Bobby, "What's your name boy?"

There was a pause, then Sylus said, "I don't think they can talk Momma."

"Of course, they can talk."

She asked again, "What's your name Boy?"

Shaking, Bobby answered, "Bobby."

Then she looked at me, "What's your name?"

"Jimmy Ma'am."

She looked at Bobby, and pointed at him, "You look familiar."

She thought for a moment, then said, "Ain't you Buddy Olindorf's boy?"

Bobby said, "Yes Ma'am."

"Well, we are the Weber's. Your Granddaddy, before he died, rest his soul; And now your Daddy, hires my boys, Billy John and Sylus, to help him haul sometimes. Mr. Olindorf is a very nice man. What with the money he pays, and the money I get from my late husband's military retirement, the money that Billy John, and Sylus gets from their military disability, we make a pretty good piece of money."

When we heard that Mrs. Weber knew and liked Bobby's father and grandpa; Bobby and I were relieved. Suddenly, everything seemed much different. I was relieved that we probably, were not going to get eaten.

She paused then asked, "What are you boys doing way out here?"

Bobby said, "We were just exploring Mrs. Weber."

"Oh, just call me Ellie."

Billy John said, "Yeah we just saw them out on the trail when we was huntin' rabbits. Brought them here so they wouldn't get soaked in the rain. There was another one, but he got spooked and run off. I hope he found shelter from the rain. It's going hard out there right now."

Ellie went in the house. When she returned, she had a towel for each of us so we could dry ourselves. She went back inside. She returned with a pitcher of sweet tea and paper cups for us. The next time she left and retuned she offered us a big bowl of popcorn. We all said "thank you" and started eating. I could smell and hear that she was popping more popcorn. That was the best sweet tea, and popcorn I ever tasted.

POW Camps

We all sat on the benches at the table on the porch. The rain cooled the temperature quite a bit, it actually began to feel really comfortable sitting there. Ellie was in a talkative mood, maybe she liked the company. Even though we were only nine, she talked as though we were older, and could relate, to what she was telling us.

Bobby asked, "I noticed you were limping Billy John, what happened to your leg?"

Before Billy John could answer, Ellie proudly said, "That happened in Korea, both of my boys are heroes." Ellie gave a big smile, "They are very shy and probably would never tell you. Sylus received a Purple Heart. Billy John was awarded the Purple Heart, and the Bronze Star, when he and Sylus was in Korea."

Bobby asked, "Do you have other children?

"Yeah, the boys have an older sister, Mable. I don't talk about her much. She ran away with, and married one of them Nazis, from the POW camp, after his release, when the war was over.

I was surprised. I asked, "Did you say a Prisoner of War camp, was here in Louisiana?"

Ellie said, "Oh yes, there was one right off North Carolina St; there were Italian POW's there too."

I said, "That is right down the street from my Granny. She lives on South Carolina."

Ellie was a wealth of information, and I could not wait to get home and ask Granny all about that POW camp. Once the rain stopped, Bobby and I said our goodbye's, and ran down the path until we got to our bikes. We walked our bikes down the path, until we made it to the road.

Once to the road we were away, like the wind. We said goodbye and split company at the paved road. Bobby rode east toward his house, and I rode west toward Granny's.

Saying Goodbye

When I arrived at Granny's she told me that my Dad had called and told her that he and my mother were coming to pick me up on August 18, the day after my birthday. This was only two weeks away. The week before my birthday would be the big game, against the Eagles which would decide the championship. Only three weeks remaining, of the coolest summer I ever had.

I asked Granny about the POW camp, for Nazi's and Italians, down off North Carolina St. Granny told a story of grievance the black people in Hannibal and Louisiana had concerning the POW's. The war prisoners, often were treated better, and respected more, by white people in Louisiana and Hannibal, than were black people. They also worked jobs, that towns people could have had. The prisoners, were used as free labor, by businessmen in town and on the farms.

Granny explained that black people were upset, their relatives were fighting and dying in the war. Black soldiers were fighting in the war, while back at home, black people were being systematically and legally discriminated against. It was a different perspective from Ellie's, but definite confirmation, and verification that the POW camps, in Louisiana and Hannibal did exist. It was always great to talk about things with Granny.

When my father arrived to pick me up, it was hard to say goodbye to everyone. I said goodbye to Mikey and his parents. I was jealous, they were all going to remain with Granny, for one more week, but I had to go to South Dakota.

It was hard to say goodbye to My Aunt Lucy and Uncle Kenny, Mikey's Mom and Dad. I hugged Granny for a long time and shook hands with Granddad Clifford. Bobby rode his bike over, so that he could say goodbye. I knew that I would really miss Bobby. I did not realize, at the time, that I would never see Bobby again.

After my move to South Dakota, Granny wrote to me, and told me that Bobby's dad took a job in St. Louis, and the whole family moved there. Bobby and I completely lost touch. I remember thinking a lot about our adventures and baseball experience. I was so sad that, my best summer ever, was ending.

Curled up in the corner of the backseat. While my father, mother, and I rode away in the 1956, Ford station wagon, I secretly cried. I cried from sorrow of, what I thought would be, impending loneliness, and heartbreak.

I had no way of knowing that in the great north of South Dakota, I would meet and befriend Danny. Danny and I would have great fun exploring, Ellsworth Air Force Base. I did not know that At Ellsworth, I would fall madly in love with Patty, a girl who sat across the room from me in class. I did not know, that I would receive a brand new bike, for my 10th birthday, and become a "big star" (In my own mind) on the next level of little league baseball.

Back in Louisiana, we lost the Championship game by one run. Even though we lost, and summer league was over, Coach said it was the best game we played all season. The players felt a sense of accomplishment and achievement even though we lost the game. The experiences and friendships we developed were awesome.

In this current moment, as the country and the world, struggles through extreme difficulty. We all are battling COVID-19, having to face the unpleasant realities of systemic racism, and feeling the beginnings, of the effects, and impending devastation of climate change, I sometimes think back to a more innocent time, in a kid's mind. I think of the experiences surrounding the championship, as a time to remember, and even though, that summer with Granny, in Louisiana, Missouri, are long gone, it was a summer to remember.

We Are All In This Together

It was a commercial on television, referencing COVID-19, **WE ARE ALL IN THIS TOGETHER**, that caused me to remember the Guard. I realized that, in boot camp and in training classes after boot camp, it was being driven into us recruits, that we should pull together, cooperate, and collaborate to help each other be successful in our efforts to complete missions.

That message reminded me of my first duty station, during my four years in the military, aboard the U.S. Coast Guard Cutter Owasco. Our missions were almost always ones to help people, and to help keep America safe. But even now, over 40 years later, that television commercial brings that message, from the Guard, alive within me again.

The motto in the United States Coast Guard is Semper Paratus, always prepared, ready for any emergency. I thought I was being very clever, as a young Seaman, fresh out of boot camp, when I was talking to my Coastie buddies.

When my buddies would ask, "Are you ready to go?" In reference to leaving for one place or other.

I would answer, "I am in the Guard Baby; like the battery, I am everready!"

Everyone would crack up almost every time I said that, probably more because it was extremely corny, rather than actually humorous. To get the joke, a person had to be familiar, with the popular Duracell battery, and later the Energizer Bunny commercials. But, at the same time, being ready was our mindset. We had an unspoken bond that in any situation, we could count on each other. We considered ourselves to be in any and all situations together, one for all and all for one. However, it took us, especially me, a while to get there, to really understand.

I arrived to report for duty aboard the 254 foot, high endurance cutter Owasco (WHEC-39), a United States Coast Guard Vessel, just a few weeks after graduation from Radar School. I remember thinking that the red, white, and blue strip down the side of the bow was beautiful. The Owasco was the biggest water vessel I had ever boarded in my life. Although I realized that the Owasco was small, in comparison to the big Navy ships, it looked pretty huge, to me at the time. As I saluted the officer on deck to board, I felt very proud to be serving my country.

Once aboard, I put my things away at the bunk and locker, I had been assigned. I went to the mess hall to get something to eat and see if I could meet some people. The mess hall looked like a small cafeteria with a metal service line shelf, and seating for about forty people. Round portal like windows were along one side of the room and the ceiling was low, about 8 feet from the floor. Two doors, one on each side of the room, were secured open, probably because the ship was docked, for repairs and replenishing, to prepare for the next mission.

There was only one person in the room. I could see by the brown uniform he wore, and the insignia on his collar that he was a Senior Chief Petty Officer. His hat was kind of plopped on top of thick, curly, red hair. His face was thick, puffy, and round. He had a bushy red beard peppered with gray. He was handsome in a weathered kind of way.

The visor of his hat slanted down to slightly shade his dark green eyes. He looked to be about 5'9", if he were standing. He was of medium build, with broad shoulders and a prominent neck. The chief looked as if he was slightly smiling all of the time. He looked to be having a burger and fries for lunch.

I introduced myself to the Chief, and he told me just to call him either Senior Chief, Chief Denny, Chief, or just Denny. I asked him what the guys on the ship called him. He joked saying that, when he could hear them, they mostly called him Chief Denny. He said that they probably had more, "colorful" names when they thought, he was out of earshot. He said all the officers called him Senior Chief.

I discovered later that although there were other Chiefs on board, he was the highest ranked, enlisted man on the ship. Further, he was one of, just a few guys in the Guard, who had earned the rank of Senior Chief. I decided to go with Chief Denny, I thought that I, would look foolish if, it seemed that I did not honor his accomplishments.

Chief Denny was a wealth of information. He explained that, in about two weeks, he would retire, after 25 years in the Guard. Chief Denny explained that he was from Maine, and had served on three ships since he graduated boot camp; one ice breaker out of the Great Lakes, one cutter out of Hawaii, but most of his time was spent on the Owasco. He was transferred to the Owasco in 1966 and had been on the ship since. We got along so well, that we met for lunch every day, until it was time for him to depart.

Chief Denny did two tours in Nam on two different ships. He had some horror stories and some heart wrenching stories to tell as well. Chief Denny gave me good advice every time we talked. One practical piece of advice that eventually helped save me, was how to wrestle with sea sickness.

I explained to Chief Denny, in all of my youthful bravado, and overblown attitudes of invulnerability, "I am not too worried, about getting seasick, I rarely get sick."

Chief Denny asked, "Being from Kansas City, have you ever been out to sea, where you cannot see land anywhere?"

I said, "No, but it doesn't sound like a big deal though."

"Well, my friend; you might be surprised."

Chief Denny smiled widely, then said, "If you do happen to get seasick, remember, always eat something at every meal - force yourself to eat saltine crackers, if you have no appetite, never miss a duty watch, and carry a rubber bucket every place you go."

He smiled widely, "And please, clean the bucket after every use."

I chuckled a little and very nonchalantly said, "Right, thanks, I will."

Chief Denny told me that there were a compliment of 13 officers and 121 enlisted men on board, any time the ship is ready to head out to sea. He explained that the ship usually goes out to sea for 30 days at a time; then returns to New London to dock for 30 days. He explained that during weekends, when docked, the ship is on "Holiday Routine." When we are docked, most of the men on the Radar crew, worked 8:00AM to 12:00PM and have an open grille in the galley; everyone cooks on his own. That is where I learned to cook for myself.

There was a skeleton crew, when I first arrived, but every week a few more guys showed up, returning from leave. I met more of the crew, each week as they returned. I met the leader of the radar team crew, First Class Petty Officer Breshard.

The two of us got along great. After about two weeks with us, Petty Officer Breshard matched all six of the radar crew members, so that each of us had a partner. My partner was a guy from northern Connecticut named, Tom Sully. We were the same rank, E4 and became great friends.

The week before the ship was set to depart everyone assigned to the ship had returned from leave and people were making sure they took time to say goodbye to Chief Denny, and to wish him well. I was sad to say farewell to Chief Denny, but glad that he was retiring, while still young.

Chief Denny had plans to become a Harbor Pilot in Portland Maine, and work until he retired again. He had it all planned out, he joined the Guard when he was 18, right out of high school, would retire at 43, and would work 20 years as a Harbor Pilot and retire again at 63. Almost all of the men in Chief Denny's family had been Harbor Pilots, including his father, his uncles, both his grandfathers, and Chief Denny's older brother.

That final week before we launched Shardi, that's what everyone called Petty Officer Breshard, led several drills every day. He wanted to make sure everyone, especially me, was ready to go, when the time came for us to launch.

I was the rookie. "The Rook," short for rookie. Rook became my nickname on the team. Just before it was time to pull out, Shardi named Sully and me as the first team. He matched us, because

Sully had been on the ship (two years) longer than the rest of us, and I was "The Rook." After watching all of the drills, Shardi told everyone that he considered Sully, and me to be the top two on the Radarmen Teams, so we were named, team one.

Shardi told us all to remember, radar was the eyes of the ship and once on mission, "we are all in this together." During the departure briefing, Shardi confirmed that each team would have 4 hours on duty; 8 hours off duty shifts. Each of the three teams, would be on watch twice every 24 hours. Shardi put names to the schedule by saying that the teams would rotate in order; Team One would start, Team Two would follow, last would be Team Three. When the ship departed on my first mission, I was very excited and Sully and I had the first watch.

The XO (Executive Officer - second in command on the ship) directed our departure from the harbor, under the watchful eye of the captain. Shardi was in CIC (the radar room of the Combat Information Center) with Sully and me. Once underway, our job was to report, to the bridge, The precise location of all surface contacts within range of the ship, on the ocean and in the air.

I learned later that the XO, and the Captain were rarely, on the bridge at the same time, unless some serious situation happens. Likewise, Shardi would not regularly be in the CIC with a Radar Team. But, I discovered, that when the ship departed a port, or was docking at a port, Shardi was in CIC as support if needed. Further, throughout a mission, Shardi would intermittingly visit a team on watch to "keep his eye on the situation." Sully told me that Shardi did not micro-manage, but was a great advocate for the Radar Teams.

As the ship moved out of the harbor to enter the open sea, we were into the Atlantic Ocean very quickly. The ride was smooth, but to my surprise I was already feeling a little Queasy.

I was instantly concerned that I might be experiencing seasickness. I had never been seasick before, so the feelings were a mystery. The more the ship moved out into the ocean, the more uncomfortable I felt.

I was too embarrassed to say something to Sully or Shardi, about how I was feeling. They would really think of me as, "The Rook," if I could not even make it past the outer buoy without getting seasick.

I had three hours remaining on my watch and I was determined to hold back the vomit somehow. I realized that if I could remain as still as possible, not move much, I might be able to fight back the urge to regurgitate. Shardi moved from CIC to the bridge, to look out the windows, to view the beauty of the open ocean.

The CIC room had no windows and was dark inside, therefore Sully and I could not see the water. Once under way the overhead lights in the CIC, were turned off. The boards, screens and scopes, inside the room were luminated in green and red, and without the overhead lights, became very bright and made them much easier to view. The lightning and atmosphere in the room had the feel of a, dark room, used to develop film.

Once Shardi was gone to the bridge, I felt I had to tell Sully how I was feeling, he told me to go to the Head (Restroom) which was one flight of stairs down from CIC. Holding back the urge to throw-up, I sprinted down those stairs. As soon as I entered the stall, the vomit came hard.

Everything I had for breakfast came up. The smell was awful, but a positive was, my aim was good and most of the vomit hit inside the toilet Stool. After I finished, I cleaned up the area. Standing there in the head, I thought of Chief Denny. Suddenly, I did not feel so cocky anymore, about being invulnerable to seasickness.

I remembered about the bucket. I looked in the utility closet that was in the corner and found a rubber bucket, probably placed there, to use for cleaning the area. As sick as I felt, I wanted badly to go laydown in my bunk. I remembered Chief Denny again, he told me, "Don't miss a watch."

I went back to CIC and made good use of the bucket, many more times, during the three hours remaining on my watch. I could sense that Sully felt empathy for me, but it did not stop his thinly muzzled laughter, every time I gave a big heave. At that moment I was a source of entertainment for Sully.

When my watch was over, I headed straight to my bunk. The positive was that the only place, I felt would provide some refuge from the seasickness, and the feeling that I would die at any moment, was the idea of laying on my back, on my bunk. Once the back of my head hit the pillow, I instantly felt better, not great, but at least better. I kept the bucket next to my bed, just in case.

I was sick every single day, some days worse than others, but I would get up, shower, and go to my watch. The bucket was a constant festoon with me. After my watch, I went to the mess hall and asked the cook for a sleeve of saltine crackers, he smiled knowingly, and gave me a whole box of crackers.

For thirty days, I carried that bucket everywhere I went. I ate saltine crackers, sometimes adding peanut butter, for every meal and never missed a watch. Like stories of old, where sea going men, would hold off their desires, for the sirens, of Greek mythology tempting the sailors, to throw themselves into destruction, My urge at the time, was to go to bed. I fought that and dream, that however, was an endless battle.

Everyone on the team offered to stand part of my watch for me. Shardi even made a possible schedule modification. The change in the schedule had each person on the Radar Team, standing one hour of my watch for me, that way I could fight through the sickness. I remembered Chief Denny. Therefore, I thanked everyone. My crackers, peanut butter, my bucket, and I never missed a watch.

I really appreciated the way the guys were willing to step up, to help me through the seasickness situation. We were all together, "one for all and all for one." That was a great feeling, knowing that everyone had my back; I felt fortified.

By the third voyage my body had gotten somewhat use to being on the ocean. I still experienced sickness, but nowhere near the intensity of the first mission. My body responded much better with each successive mission.

On the third mission, after we had been out to sea for a week, the new Electrician's Mate, who was making his first sea voyage, got seriously seasick. His name was Calico, he was from Idaho, and had never been on a ship.

Calico started vomiting like crazy from the first day out. After vomiting the first time, the first thing he did was lay down on his bunk. Calico never actually made a watch. He remained in bed all day, every day. Calico stopped eating on the second day.

Calico had the dry heaves after the third day. There was nothing left in his stomach to vomit, the Corpsmen gave him medicine, but he vomited the medicine, they gave him shots, but it did not help him. He began to just vomit blood, then some mucous, then he had the dry heaves, nothing came up.

The Corpsmen were trying to get him to get out of bed, but he was just yelling and cussing. He screamed at them to just let him die. I felt bad for Calico.

When I could hear his yelling echoing through the sleeping quarters, all I could do was think to myself, "Thank God for Chief Denny." I thought to myself, "There, but by the grace of God, go I." The next day, a Coast Guard helicopter landed on the fantail and they carried him away.

Sully and I went out onto the outside area of the bridge to watch the helicopter land and take-off. Sully explained that the helicopter was a MH - 60 Jayhawk. I knew nothing about helicopters, but Sully knew all about Coast Guard helicopters. Sully told me, while we were watching, that he first wanted to fly rescue helicopters, but did not qualify for that training. His test scores were not at the right level.

As the helicopter was landing and taking off, Sully talked me through the angles needed, and explained that the pilot had to have a sturdy hand, as he eased the copter onto the deck. We watched as the seamen carried Calico on the stretcher to the sliding doors on the Jayhawk, and lifted him into the opening to two crewmembers on the copter.

We continued watching until the copter, glided away as it left the ship. I felt sad for Calico, as I saw the helicopter take him away. As they flew off into the distance, I thought to myself, "That could have been me. Thank God for Chief Denny."

During the 30 days off after the first, second, and third mission I spent lots of time hanging out with the guys, on the Radar Team, and lots of alone time exploring New London. I often drove my 1965.5, candy apple red, Ford Mustang to the beach. There were many gorgeous girls to observe, while they were doing "at the beach stuff."

Some of the girls were playing volleyball, some were swimming, but most of them were just sunning themselves. One of the girls caught my eye. She smiled at me a few times, but I was way too shy, to actually talk to her.

I did, do some "detective work," and discovered she was a Junior at Connecticut College. But, by the time I got up the nerve, to take a trip up to the college, it was time for another mission. Therefore, I just settled for spending time walking over to the book store, and browsing through the book stacks.

Once in a while, I would drive over to the Coast Guard Academy. The Academy was located just between, New London and Groton Connecticut. I liked to go to the book store there, and just soak up the military college atmosphere. I toyed with the idea of finishing up my college career there, after my first tour of duty.

During my time with the guys, there were lots of conversations about Chief Denny, all the guys seemed to miss him. To me he was my role model. Sully had worked with Chief Denny, more and longer, than anyone else on the Radar Team; they had been great pals.

Sully and Chief Denny corresponded with each other at least once a month since Chief Denny retired. Chief Denny liked to keep up with everyone, and Sully kept him informed about us. Likewise, Sully told us about Chief Denny's activities.

I especially liked the story about Chief Denny being aboard the Owasco during the involvement with the Market Time Units, in 1968 Vietnam. The Market Time Units operation, was a joint mission, that included U.S Navy aircraft, destroyer escort radar picket ships, ocean minesweepers, swift boats, and Vietnamese Navy Junk Force craft. Also assisting were 82-foot, and high - endurance Coast Guard Cutters, one of which was the Owasco. The main mission was for the Market Time Units to keep the communists from sneaking men, arms, and other supplies into the Republic of Vietnam.

Because of his involvement in the operation Chief Denny along with the rest of the crew of the Owasco received Navy Commendation medals and were cited in letters of commendation by the commander of the 7th Naval Fleet.

The Owasco conducted 17 Naval Gunfire Support missions, fired 1,330 rounds of 5-inch ammunition, destroyed 18 bunkers, and 550 meters of enemy supply trails. The medical crew also treated 432 Vietnamese civilians. In other words, Chief Denny and his shipmates on the Owasco exceeded the results of all other vessels in Squadron Three.

I loved that story and whenever there was some down time, someone was regularly asking Sully to tell the story again. The story to me was another example of working together to solve a problem or complete a mission. I thought about Chief Denny often, liked his calm manner, and tried to remember all of his suggestions, about what to do when at sea. He was definitely, my "Coast Guard hero."

It became part of my routine to buy four or five books the Friday before the ship departed for a mission. I became an avid reader during my time on the ship. Reading took my mind off of seasickness. I read more books, while I was stationed on the Owasco, than I had read, during all of my high school and college days put together. Being at sea was conducive to reading and thinking, plus the fact Chief Denny was a huge proponent of reading.

The first three missions, were child's play when compared to what happened on the fourth mission. I was excited to see how I would do on the fourth mission out to sea. A typical mission for the crew of the Owasco was to travel to a position in the Atlantic Ocean, and patrol a 210 square mile area, for approximately 28 to 30 days. While patrolling the area the crew of the Owasco obtained meteorological and oceanographic data and information. The Owasco also served as a navigation beacon for passing aircraft and offered accurate information about position, course, speed, and up to date weather forecasts.

I had purchased five books to read during the fourth mission. By the time we made it to the

Ocean Station, I had already started my first book. I was prepared for a quiet 28 to 30 days mission. Everything was quiet the first three weeks.

During the days, on my times off, I read books I brought with me, and I watched the guys go swimming in the ocean. I never went swimming in the ocean; swimming was not my strong suit. I was sure sharks were out there waiting for me to jump in, so they could eat parts of my body.

Sully, on the other hand, was a crazed person, he loved to participate in such an endeavor. He was always trying to get me to join him and the other lunatics who were engaging in such activities. Ok, yes. It was very cool watching the dolphins and whales from time to time, but I was certain that the sharks were there, lurking, beneath the water, waiting on me to jump in, so they could have lunch.

When the fourth week rolled around, almost everyone was ready to head back toward port. It started at night. I was an hour into my off time. I had just turned off my reading lamp, when I heard the alarms sound. I realized, I had never actually heard the alarms, sound before. It startled me. The sound reminded me of a European bomb alarm, and police siren, in a world war II movie. I saw a bunch of guys scurrying around, then out of the sleeping quarters.

I heard someone yell, "What the heck is going on?"

A voice replied as guys were running down the aisles. "There is a fire in the laundry, come on they need help fast."

I jumped out of bed, put on my pants, shoes and a heavy shirt and followed the stream of guys running. When I got to the laundry room, the damage control guys were busy working. They were moving fast like a colony of giant army ants working on a project.

I could see that there was a hole about the size of a serving platter, in a fancy China setting, in the hull of the ship. It was a good thing the hole was high near the ceiling. Not as much water, as could have been, was being taken on. But I could see, it was gushing in faster than anyone liked.

I could see, what had happened. There had been an electrical short, of some sort, in one of the dryers. The explosion had caused a fire, and one of the pipes burst and slammed into the wall creating a hole. Water pushing through made the hole larger.

The Chief, for the damage control guys, told everyone to back away so that his guys could work. The hole was in a peculiar spot that made it difficult for the guys to reach. As the damage control guys were working there was trouble on the bridge.

The XO awakened the Captain. There was a huge Russian tanker, about three times the size of the Owasco, headed for us. The tanker looked as if it was on a collision course with us.

We changed course, but every time we changed course, so did the tanker. Suddenly, the Captain called Sully. The Captain ordered Sully, to get Radar Team one, in the Con (Con was short for CIC) now! The word came over the intercom for Radar Team One, to report to the Con ASAP.

Just as I was leaving, I felt the ship slam into something. It felt like we hit a stone wall. Everyone stumbled falling against the wall and some fell to the floor. I discovered later it was a huge wave of water.

As I was on my way to the CIC, I heard the chief of the damage control guys yell to his guys, "We have got to kill that fire Men. We need someone to get over the side to seal the breach, from the outside. This hole has to be sealed from both sides."

It was Dominik who spoke up to volunteer, "I'll go."

The Chief turned to the other damage control guys and said, "I need three men to assist Dominik?"

All of the remaining Damage Control guys moved forward raising their hands to volunteer. The Chief pointed to three of them, and all four moved into action.

I moved as quickly as I could as the ship tossed and dipped. The weather had turned to a rainy, windy storm, a nor'easter of tremendous strength was suddenly upon us. As I entered the CIC, Sully was already there.

As the storm raged on the outside, a storm inside my stomach also began to rage. Radar Team Three briefed us as to the surface contact. As they were talking, I retrieved my bucket from the corner. The ship was tossing and turning, as I luckily hit the center of the bucket with my first involuntary discharge.

Once both Sully and I, were in the room, Radar Team Three, departed to make room for Sully and me (CIC could only hold about three people comfortably. Sully took the screen and I took the table, to graph and chart. The tanker direction, speed, and distance had to be determined. The tanker was not close enough to be seen by the necked eye, only by radar.

The Captain's voice coming over the "All Call," sounded with an intensity in his voice, which I had never heard, as he said Code Yellow. Suddenly, Shardi burst through the bridge door.

The Captain asked, "Where are they Shardi?"

Shardi said, "I just got here Sir, Team One has the Con."

Sully said, "Petty officer Sully and "The Rook," here Sir, there are two bogies, not one, but two Sir."

The Captain said, "Dammit! What the Hell do they think they are doing?"

Sully said some locations to me, and I placed the indicators for the two bogies on the board. I was nervous, very nervous. I drew a few lines and vectors then said, "Constant baring decreasing range on bogie one. Bogie two also, constant baring decreasing range. They are coming at us from two different directions."

The Captain yelled to the engine room Chief, "Chief, we are going to have to out run these two butt heads! Let's get on our horses." The Captain said to the communications officer, Lieutenant Balcher, "find out if there is a carrier in the area. Maybe we need to have a couple of jets swing by those Knuckle heads!"

I suggested a redirection of the ship to the bridge, that would avoid the collision. Every time I made a suggestion for change of direction the Russian tankers, also changed direction. As the storm raged, the tankers were baring down on the Owasco.

Shardi looked at the board and reviewed my calculations then said, "These bastards are trying to ram us." Shardi went over to take a look at the scope and said, "If they ram us, we are goners.

Those tankers are huge, we will never survive, and no one will ever find us in this storm."

Up on deck, Dominic jumped over the side of the ship, and repelled down the side, with the equipment he needed in the bag, that hung over his shoulder and was secured to his waist. Dominic's three helpers assisted him as the, very cold and wet, wind and rain, flailed against them.

The three damage control guys, had secured themselves to the ship with ropes, to keep them from getting washed off the deck, and into the turbulent water. The ship was tossing and rocking side to side, down, then up in response to the hectic wave action. The three damage control guys, frantically tried to hang onto the ropes that helped secure Dominic.

Dominic held on with one hand as he pulled down the face shield then began welding. His intentions were to weld a metal plate to the hull of the ship. The idea was that he would use the metal plate, as a temporary fix to cover the hole, in the hull. He explained to me later that it was like "trying to fix a flat tire, while the car is moving." When the ship tossed in the weather and against the waves, the wind slammed Dominic into the side of the ship multiple times.

The three other damage control guys, struggled to keep Dominic from being pulled into the water. This was all happening, while the other damage control guys were below deck, trying to get the fire under control. We all realized that we were in a Hell of a predicament. I have got to tell you, I was really scared.

Looking at the radar screen, with concern in his voice, Sully said, "We are headed into a second storm that is coming, aft, right off the tail-end of the first storm."

I said, "What! Another storm?"

Shardi told us that when he was on the bridge the engines were trying to go 15 knots forward, but the storm was moving the ship 15 knots backward. He told us that engineering was in the "All hands on deck" mode. Everyone in engineering was at work, on duty trying to keep the engines going against the strain of the storm.

Shardi told us, as if I needed one more frightening thing to happen, if we lost the engine in this storm, we wouldn't have to worry about the Russians, we would be sucked up into the huge waves. I had never been so scared in all of my life. I did not see, a way out of this situation.

I said, "Is the Skipper calling for help?"

Shardi was being realistic, "Who could he call to come in this storm? I think communications is down, right now anyway. We have to find a way out of this ourselves. You guys work the scope and the board. Be ready to give us direction as soon as this storm breaks."

Shardi turned to leave. He said he was going to the bridge to help with the communication situation.

I was feeling seasick, but I had stopped having the urge to vomit. I felt weak, I knew, I had to fight through, to help get us out of this mess. The ship was moving side to side.

But what really got me was, that when the bow was forced straight up, into the air by the water, then slammed straight down, as a new wave came under the ship. That action tossed people and anything not secured, around the rooms into the bulkheads. It was like the fastest, scariest roller coaster ride, ever made. The wind was so hard, and the noise created was so loud, it was like the sound effects in some horrific horror movie. To this day I refuse to go on another rollercoaster ride.

I wondered about the fire in the laundry, but figured, it had been put out by then. What was really on my mind was Dominik. Dominik had volunteered, to jump over the side of the ship, to fix a hole, during a killer storm. I thought to myself, "Really? You have got to be kidding me!"

I admired Dominik's courage. I realized I had not spent much time getting to know Dominik, or any of the other damage control guys. I had just heard that they were very close-knit, and kind of dare-devilish types. They liked to ski the black runs, with moguls, together on the ski sloops, the faster the better. I had seen Dominik in the mess area, a few times, said hello, but that was about it.

Just as I thought it was all over, two giant waves hit the ship in close succession. The ship rocked side to side and seemed to float up into the air and out of the water. The bow dove into the water and a huge amount of water swept across the deck and the bridge area. I hoped Dominik and his team made it inside before that happened. I did not think anyone could have survived that, if they were not inside.

We were all praying after that last blast of water. It felt like the ship would split in half. But, just as the ship came up out of the water, the storm subsided almost as quickly as it had come.

The waters began to calm. Sully said that the Russian tankers had disappeared from the radar screen. The engines were moving the ship evenly as we moved easily through the calming water. I never knew, what happened to the tankers. We did realize that they had probably been up to no good. They probably wanted there to be no account of them being where they were. They probably had contraband cargo, that they did not want discovered.

The captain announced that we would return to port immediately. The engine room, put the ship at 15 knots, and the ship cruised toward New London. The repairs began while we were still at sea. It took us two days to reach the port. I think we were all happy to dock that day.

The next day almost everyone who had leave, took leave. I did not go home, because it would have been a long trip, there and back, to Kansas City, so I decided to just remain onboard.

I saw Dominik in the mess area, when I went to get a glass of ice cold milk. I walked over to him, said hello, and told him how impressed I was with his courage. I explained that I was in awe, when he jumped over the side of the ship, during that storm, to fix the hole. Dominik just smiled, and looked down at the table. Dominik was friendly, but very shy, and not talkative.

Dominik was "movie star handsome," he had thick black curly hair, somewhat longish. He had an endless battle, brushing his hair out of his face. He had a dark, kind of olive color complexion. Girls at the beach were drawn to him, they said he looked like a Greek God.

None of them had a chance though, Dominik, number one, was very shy, and number two, had a girlfriend, he intended to marry, back home. The ironic part though, is that Dominik was actually of Greek heritage. The other damage control guys kidded him by calling him "Kratos" (Greek God of strength and power) or just "Tos" for short. Dominik was about 5'5" and heavily muscled; he could be found in the gym, when the ship was docked, working out, early almost every morning,.

I asked, "Isn't your home somewhere in Connecticut?"

"Yeah, I was born and raised in Milford."

"Don't you have a girlfriend back home?"

"Yeah, Shelley."

"I don't understand, why are you not on your way home."

"I'm a little low on cash at the moment."

"Well how far is Milford from New London?"

"About 60 miles."

"I have my car, so what if I just drive you there. When you are ready to come back, after a few days, just call, and I will come pick you up?"

Dominik looked at me seemingly shocked, that I would make such an offer. He did not answer my question. He simply stared at me.

He asked, "Are you serious?"

I asked, "Could you be ready in an hour?"

Dominic and I were on the road within the hour. I had no idea where Milford is, in relation to New London. When I reported to the ship, fresh out of Radarman School, from Governors Island New York, it was the first time I had ever been to Connecticut. This was an adventure for me.

Dominik and I had a nice ride to Milford. The tree filled landscape was beautiful. Along the way we talked about baseball, his family, and Shelly. I learned a lot about Dominik on that trip. One thing was, Dominik was not much of a talker, until you got him started. Once started, Dominik was a talking machine.

I discovered that Dominik's last name was Papadopoulos. He had four brothers, two older and one younger. His mom and dad had immigrated to America, a month before he was born. His mom and dad, wanted him to be an American citizen, born in America. Dominik was born two days after the family landed in America.

According to Dominik, his dad was super patriotic, a diehard Navy veteran. Dominik said his dad was kind of embarrassing, when Dominik's friends were visiting, with his bravado Navy talk. His dad had retired, from his nuclear submarine duties, at his final duty station in Groton Connecticut. Ironically, he retired in the town adjacent, to New London, where Dominik was currently based.

Dominik said that Shelly thought his father was much more adorable than annoying. When Dominik talked about Shelly, I could see how much he loved her. She seemed to be the joy of his life.

Dominik explained that he met Shelly at the student center when he was at college. He said that he saw her sitting at a table alone studying, having a muffin and hot chocolate for breakfast.

He was on his way back to the dorm, after his workout in the weight room, at the athletic center. Dominik did not usually stop by the student center, at that time of day. But for some reason, he was really thirsty, for a fountain Coke that day. Shelly caught his eye, and Dominik could not keep himself from looking toward her. She was beautiful.

He said that he finally got up the nerve, to go over and introduce himself to her. He walked over to the table and started to introduce himself. When she looked up, she said, "You don't recognize me do you?"

Dominik said he took a deeper look. He asked her if she was Diego's sister. Dominik said that he and Diego were on the baseball team together in high school. Dominik explained that Shelly, came to the games sometimes. He never actually talked to her. But he did have the biggest crush on her. But Shelly was two years older.

Dominik knew that the age thing was a show stopper in the high school culture. It was perfectly ok, for the boy to be a year or maybe even two years older; but not for girls. Totally sexist thinking, but that was high school.

Things were different in college. Dominik said, once he discovered the, romantic feelings were mutual. After the meeting at that table, in the student center, they were never emotionally apart again.

Dominik also told me all about his favorite team, the Yankees. I, of course, had to stand up, for the Cardinals and Royals, the two MLB teams in Missouri. Most interesting though, was when Dominik talked about his high school athletic career.

Dominik was a three sport letterman. He was a three time state wrestling champion in the 120, 126, and 145 pound weight classes. Dominik also played, strong safety, on the football team, and starting catcher on the baseball team. I could see that "my man Tos" was a stud athlete in high school.

Dominik also wrestled for a year in college, but decided college was not for him at the time. He thought he would join the Guard, and see what he felt like after his first tour. Dominik had a year in the Guard remaining, a little while left to decide. The conversation with Dominik, made the hour and a half trip go fast.

When we arrived at his home, his mother and father, and younger brother, still in high school, all came outside to greet him, and to meet me. Looking at his mom and Dad, I saw right away where those good looks, of his came from.

Dominik's Mom and Dad said hello, behind their thick Greek accents. Dominik's brother, gave me a high five, and all three, thanked me for giving Dominik a ride home. Dominik's older brothers, lived out of state, so they were not there to see him.

I told his mom, dad, and younger brother that it was my honor to give him a ride. I explained that he was such a hero, I told how Dominik had saved everyone on the ship because of his tremendous courage. The whole family beamed with pride, as I spoke the truth (Against his objections and denials), about Dominik's heroic actions.

I told them that his life was clearly at risk. He placed everyone else's life and safety above his own. I did not say it, but I would have driven Dominik to California, if that was where he wanted to go.

Dominik's mom and dad, invited me in, and asked that I stay to have dinner with them, spend the night, and get an early start the next day. I thanked them, but declined. I explained that I wanted to get back by the evening. I reminded Dominik to call me when he was ready to return, and I would drive down and pick him up.

Dominik told me not to worry about that. He offered to pay for my gas there and back. I refused. He said he could get a ride back with a relative or friend, and he thanked me again for the ride there. Dominik's father gave me a hardy hand shake, and his mother gave me a very tight hug, and kiss on the cheek.

As I drove away, I had warm feelings about the Papadopoulos family. I decided to take a drive around the town, before I got back on the highway. Milford was south of New London, in the southern region of the state.

The downtown area had several quaint cafes and small shops, boutiques, and bookstores. The town looked like a great place for browsing. I passed a quaint little restaurant that had a sign that read "Papadopoulos Café - Authentic Greek Food."

I smiled and thought, during our entire trip to Milford, Dominik never once said anything about his family's restaurant business. Milford had plenty of big sprawling trees, and a nice beach area as well. Milford was a beautiful little town. I thought I might like to visit it again someday.

As I drove back to New London, I prayed a couple of prayers thanking God, for helping us fight, through the challenges, of that last mission. All 123 sailors and 13 officers made it back alive and well. Everyone had pitched in together. Courage was in the air.

Even though people were afraid, we all stuck together, and fought to get back to our home port. I felt proud to serve, I was glad to be serving America, among the brave souls, in the brotherhood and sisterhood of the United States Coast Guard.

At that moment, I remembered Chief Denny. I began to mentally review things he had taught me. But the most important teaching of all, was Semper Peritus! **"WE ARE ALL IN THIS TOGETHER!"** And we all, can rally around that today, to defeat COVID.

Printed in the United States
by Baker & Taylor Publisher Services